P9-EAI-884

Grandpa's Great City Tour

AN ALPHABET BOOK BY

James Stevenson

GREENWILLOW BOOKS
New York

Printed in U.S.A. First Edition 5 4 3 2 1

Library of Congress Cataloging in Publication Data
Stevenson, James, (date) Grandpa's great city tour.
Summary: Drawings portray grandpa touring the city, encountering on each page objects, animals, and people whose names begin with a particular letter of the alphabet.
[1. Alphabet. 2. Stories without words] I. Title.
PZ7.S84748Gq 1983 [E] 83-1459
ISBN 0-688-02323-1 ISBN 0-688-02324-X (lib. bdg.)

A,a
CITY
Tour

ATOR
INES

B,b

BUS
BAKERY
BANK
SIGHTSEEING
BAND BARGE

C,c
CAROUSEL

D,d

DESERT

DINING
ROOM
→

E,e
11
EXIT

ELEVATOR
SOHO
EYEGLASSES

F,f
FEATHER FACTORY
FISH
FIRE DEPT.

FRUIT
FERRY

G,g
GUARD
GUIDE BOOK

H,h

HOSPITAL
KEEP OUT-
HAUNTED
STAY AT
HOTEL
HOG'S
HOOK

HAST
BURGE
HAMBURGER
HUGE BURGER
HEFTY BURGER
HOT DOG
HONEY

I,i
J,j
JIG SAW
PUZZLE
JOKES
INK

ICE CREA
JELLYFISH
II

K,k
KETCHUP

Menu

L, l

LAUNDR
SAME DAY
U.S.
MAIL

M, m
THIS MONTH at the MUSEUM
THE MOON & MARS
SPECIAL LUNCH: MACARONI
MILK

EUM
AMMOTH
MAP

N,n
NOISE
NEWS
NATIONAL NONSENSE
NIGHT NEWS

HONK
BEEP!
SALTED
NUTS

O,o
OLIVES

P,p
PIZZA
PEANU
BUTT

POPSICLES
POPCORN

Q,q
QUIET, PLEASE
QUACK
QUACK

QUACK
?

R, r
RIVER
Restaurant

Rabbit's
Roses

S, s
SCHOOL

S
72
SLED

T,t
TURNPIKE
THRUWAY
TUNNEL
PAY TOLL

HEATRE
TICKETS
TUNA
TOOTHPASTE
TEETH
TAILO

U,u

V,v
VITAMINS
VALENTI

VOLCANO
PHARMACY
VEGETA

W,w

WELCOM

X,x
Y,y
Z,z
ALLIGATOR
AIR LINES
CITY
TOUR

YOGURT
ZERO'S
ZIPPERS

A
B
C
D
E
F
G
H
I
J
K
L
M
N
O
P
Q
R
S
T
U
V
W
X
Y
Z
abcdefg
ijklmno
qrstuv
xyz